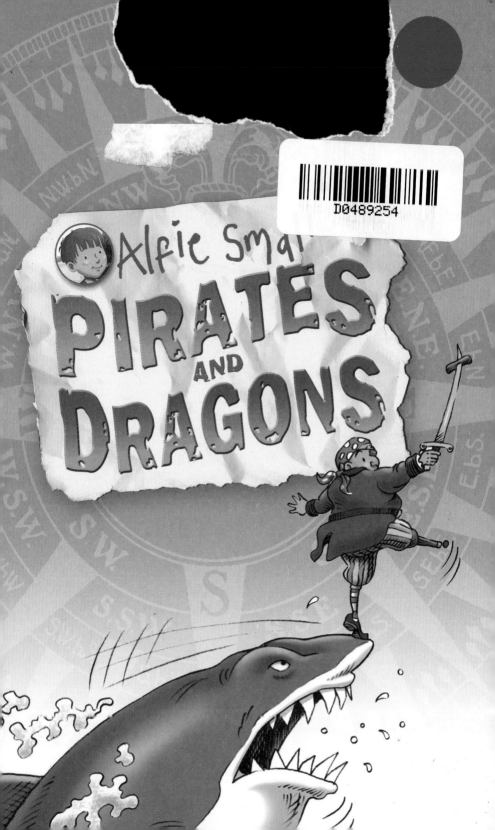

I have gone exploring. Got my rucksack. Don't worry, I'll be home in time for tea. Love, Alfie X

Here's the note I always leave for Mum before I go on another adventure

ALFIE SMALL JOURNAL 1: Pirates and Dragons
A DAVID FICKLING BOOK 978 1 849 921190

Published in Great Britain by David Fickling Books,
a division of Random House Children's Books
A Random House Group Company

This edition published 2012

1 3 5 7 9 10 8 6 4 2

DAVID FICKLING BOOKS
31 Beaumont Street, Oxford, OX1 2NP

www.kidsatrandomhouse.co.uk
www.totallyrandombooks.co.uk
www.randomhouse.co.uk

Addresses for companies within The Random House Group Limited can be found at:
www.randomhouse.co.uk/offices.htm

THE RANDOM HOUSE GROUP Limited Reg. No. 954009

A CIP catalogue record for this book is available from the British Library.

Printed in China

Photographs of Alfie's finds by Ian Rycroft. www.ianrycroft.co.uk

This is the Adventure Journal of
Alfie Small

Hobbies: Exploring and having adventures!

Things I Like: Speedboats, sea dragons
and sword fighting

Things I Hate: Wrinkly old pirates and
interfering puffins

1. All Aboard

My name is Alfie Small, and I'm a famous explorer. I have lots of dangerous adventures and always take my rucksack with me, just in case!

At the bottom of my garden, behind the rickety shed, is the special place I go exploring.

This is me →

This is my explorer's kit

The grass grows long and the weeds are tall and I never know what I might find.

Today, I pushed through the weeds . . . and found a boat floating on a small stream.

So I climbed aboard and paddled away. The stream got bigger and the water flowed faster, and soon I was racing along as fast as a speedboat.

I saw a huge boulder blocking the river. It was shaped like a dragon's head and my boat raced straight towards it. Help! I thought I was going to crash.

Dragon's head rock

Then, with an awful grinding noise, the rock began to move. A dark cave opened up like a yawning mouth, and I was swept inside.

Whoosh! I whizzed along a gloomy tunnel, holding on tight as my boat zigzagged between rocks as sharp as dragon fangs.

The water roared and my boat span round and round. Soon I couldn't tell which way was home.

Suddenly, I shot out of the tunnel and found myself floating on a choppy sea. In the distance was a small island, with a plume of smoke billowing up from behind some trees. I steered my boat towards it.

2. A Monster from the Deep!

I bobbed across the silvery surf, but I hadn't gone very far when *CRASH!* Something hit my boat from underneath.

I was thrown out of the boat

Eek! I went spinning through the air and splashed into the water. Beneath the foaming waves I saw a long, snarling snout rushing towards me.

I tried to dodge it but I was too slow,

and the next minute I was lifted out of the water on the neck of a ferocious-looking sea dragon.

He turned his head and opened his terrible jaws.

Help! I thought he was going to gobble me up in one big bite.

Yuck! I got dragon slime on my diary!

HISSSSS!

But he didn't!

"Who are you?" asked the dragon in a silky, whispery voice.

"I'm Alfie Small, the famous explorer, and you've just broken my boat," I said.

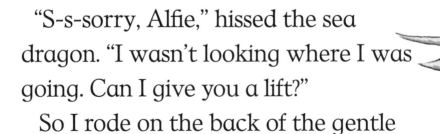

"S-s-sorry, Alfie," hissed the sea dragon. "I wasn't looking where I was going. Can I give you a lift?"

So I rode on the back of the gentle

dragon as he dived in and out of the waves, all the way to the distant island. *Yeehah!*

When we reached the rocky shore, I slid down the sea dragon's neck and said goodbye. One of his violet scales snapped off in my hand. I put it in my rucksack to show Mum, and set off to explore the craggy island.

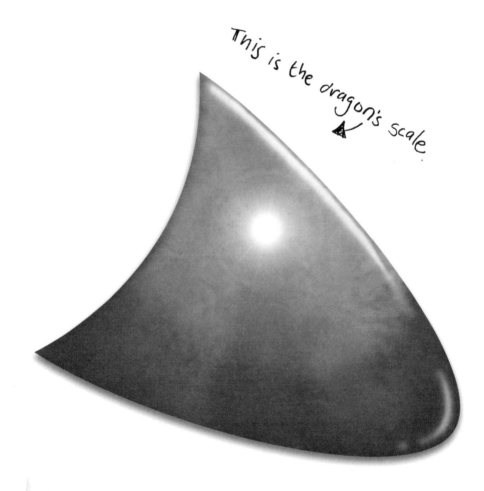

This is the dragon's scale.

3. Sizzling Sausages!

I climbed up from the beach into a leafy wood, and tiptoed quietly through the trees. The wood grew right across the middle of the small island and as I approached the shore on the far side, I heard somebody singing, very badly.

It's a pirate's life for me,
A pirate's life for me,
With the cannon's roar
And treasure galore,
It's a pirate's life for me.

I crept forward carefully. Beyond the trees, on a sandy beach, sat the most terrifying pirate you can imagine.

He had a crimson eyepatch, a carved wooden leg and a nose as knobbly as an old potato. In his wrinkled mouth was the stub of a pipe, and a fat puffin sat upon his shoulder.

The pirate was cooking. A sizzling sausage was skewered on the end of his long, curved cutlass and he was dangling it over a smoky bonfire.

Cutlass

Beside him was a big treasure chest, overflowing with gold and rubies.

I didn't like the look of him one bit, but just as I turned to sneak away, there was a loud squawk.

The Pirate

Knobbly nose

Eyepatch

Fat puffin

Pipe

Wooden leg

"Intruders, Cap'n Bonedust," screeched the fat puffin.

"Robbers!" yelled the pirate. He jumped up and charged towards me, swishing his cutlass through the air. It still had the sausage on the end, and my tummy rumbled with hunger.

"I don't want your silly old treasure,"
I cried, but Captain Bonedust wasn't
listening.

"I'll turn you into mincemeat!" he
roared.

"You don't scare me," I said, and drew
the wooden sword from my rucksack. I
rushed at him, yelling at the top of my
voice.

"I'm Alfie Small, the famous pirate-
catcher!" I cried.

4. Captured!

*C**rash!*** Our swords clashed and a mighty battle began.

Whack! The pirate's old brown pipe flew out of his mouth.

Smash, bang! The fat puffin fell off the captain's shoulder

with a squawk of alarm.

Swish, clash, wallop!

I sent the pirate's cutlass spinning from his hand.

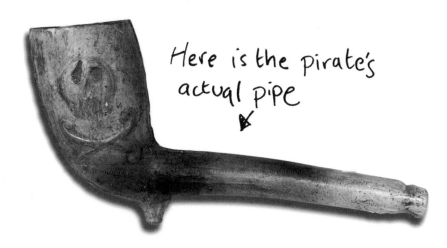

Here is the pirate's actual pipe

"Stop, Alfie. I give in," cried the captain, holding up his hands in surrender. But just then, the interfering puffin darted forward and yanked on my shoelaces. I tripped and fell, sprawling on the ground.

I hate interfering puffins

"Aha! Got you," cried the captain, and grabbed me by my collar. "It's the plank for you, you skinny scrap of seaweed."

The puffin cackled with delight. "Alfie walk the plank," he squawked.

Captain Bonedust picked up his cutlass, heaved the treasure chest onto his shoulder and marched me along the beach to his pirate galleon. It bristled with cannons, and had a huge, grinning skull carved on its prow.

As we climbed aboard, I could hear lots of shouting coming from below the deck.

"That's my horrible crew," growled Bonedust. "They told me they'd had enough of being pirates and wanted to go home to their mummies. When I refused, the cowardly curs tried to take over my ship, so I locked 'em in the hold."

"Let us out, you scurvy dog!" came their muffled cries from beneath our feet.

"Not till you've learned your lesson, sissies!" bellowed the captain, stamping his wooden leg on the floor. Then, he

fixed me with an icy stare.

"Now it's time to deal with you," he snarled.

Oh, yikes!

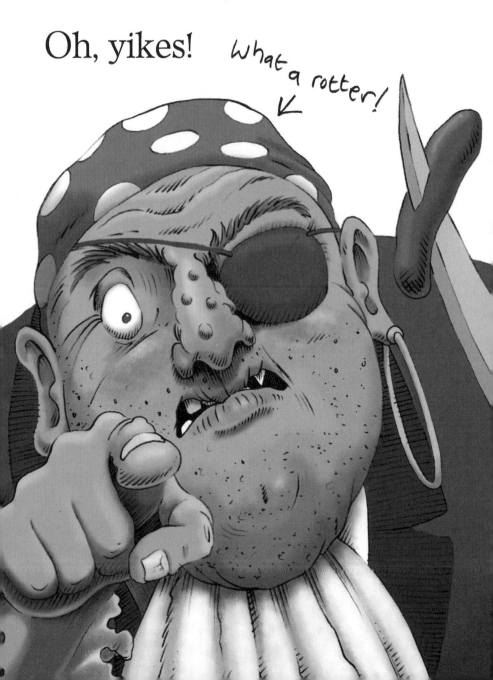

5. The Hungry Shark!

The captain forced me onto the plank.

"Look lively, you bothersome barnacle. March to the end and jump to your doom," he yelled, and jabbed me with his cutlass, which still had the greasy sausage skewered on its end.

"Ouch," I cried, and shuffled to the end of the plank. I looked down into the water. A huge, curved fin was circling the cove.

"There's a shark down there!" I gasped.

"Yes, and he's very, very hungry," chuckled Captain Bonedust. "Now, do as you're told."

"No way!" I replied.

"Then I'll come and push you in," thundered the pirate, and he strode towards me, his wooden leg going *tap, tap, tap* on the plank.

Good, I thought. That's just what I want you to do!

When he was just a step or two away, I began jumping up and down on the end of the plank. It wibbled and wobbled, and Captain Bonedust wibbled and wobbled too.

"Stop that, you slimy sea slug!" he cried, but he lost his footing and tumbled off the plank.

Charming!

Slimy sea slug ↗

Aaargh!

Bye bye, Bonedust!

"Yeark!" cried the puffin, launching himself into the sky as the captain fell, whirling his arms like a windmill in a gale!

The hungry shark opened his mighty jaws. He snapped them shut – but too soon! Captain Bonedust landed with his foot on the end of the shark's nose. He waved his cutlass about to try and keep his balance.

"Fetid fish-guts. Help me!" he bellowed.

The shark smelled the sausage on the end of the pirate's cutlass and chased after it, right across the cove and far out to sea, the fat puffin flapping after him.

"Come back, Captain," he squawked.

"Get me off here!" screamed the captain.

"You must be joking," screeched the fat little puffin as he flew around and around the pirouetting pirate, keeping well out of reach of the shark's razor-sharp teeth.

I watched until Captain Bonedust was out of sight. "Good riddance to bad rubbish!" I shouted. Then a delicious smell, from far, far away, drifted through the air. I lifted my nose and sniffed.

Rumbling tummy

I recognize that smell, I thought.
Food! My tea was ready and I knew it
was time to go home.

But how was I going to get there?

Help!

Good riddance!

6. Captain Alfie

I couldn't sail the galleon all on my own, so I rushed over to the hatchway. It was tied shut with a heavy rope. I tried to cut it with my explorer's scissors but it was much too thick, so I found a pirate's sword and sliced it in half.

The hatch flew open. A gruesome gang of hairy brigands with hooped earrings and blackened, stumpy teeth swarmed onto the deck.

What a crew—Yuck!

"Eek! Who are you?" they asked, backing away in alarm when they saw my curved cutlass. "And where's that nasty Captain Bonedust? He's been simply HORRID to us."

Captain Alfie Small,
scourge of the ocean!

Bonedust was right. His crew looked frighteningly fierce, but they were really a bunch of soppy sissies!

When I explained what had happened they gave three loud cheers and made me their new captain!

"Hooray for Alfie," they yelled, doing little tippy-toe dances all round the deck. "Bonedust wanted to keep the treasure all to himself, but now we can take it home to our mummies!"

"Yes, but you must take me home first," I ordered.

"Yes, Cap'n Alfie," they obeyed, and hauled up the anchor. But there wasn't a breath of wind. The boat wouldn't move.

What am I going to do?

Then I had an idea.

"Oh, Sea Dragon!" I cried at the top of my voice.

The hissing monster popped his head above the water.

"I need to get home for tea, but there's no wind to sail the ship," I explained.

"Easy-peasy," hissed the sea dragon with a grin. "Hold on to your hats-s-s." He took a huge breath and blew. The sails filled with wind and the galleon went skimming over the water.

"S-s-so long, Alfie," roared the sea dragon.

"Bye, Dragon," I called. "And thanks!"

The pirates steered the ship across the wide ocean until we came to rest on a muddy bank.

"Here we are, Captain Alfie. Thanks for getting rid of that horrid Captain Bonedust," said an old pirate covered in tattoos of pretty flowers. He gave me a golden doubloon from the treasure chest.

I put it in my rucksack and clambered ashore.

"Cheerio, shipmates!" I said, waving goodbye.

This is the actual doubloon

I pushed through the tall and tangled weeds on the bank, and came out from behind the shed at the bottom of my garden.

"Alfie, your tea is ready," I heard Mum call.

Mmmm, sausages! I wonder if the shark has eaten his yet? I thought, and raced up the garden path.

I am Alfie Small, the famous explorer, and I can't wait for my next amazing adventure to begin.